To girls navigating impossible standards.

50% of profits from this book is donated to Girl Up, a United Nations Foundation campaign dedicated to
empowering young girls to take action on global issues.

Printed in the United States of America

Written by Hayoung Yim
Illustrated by Marta M.

Rhyming Reason
Canada
www.rhymingreason.com

JUV039000 JUVENILE FICTION / Social Themes
JUV014000 JUVENILE FICTION / Girls & Women

ISBN 978-0-9937174-8-2

The Girl Who Said Sorry

Written by Hayoung Yim
Illustrated by Marta M

"You wear too much pink," they said;

Then, "You look too much like a boy."

So I said sorry.

They complained, "You're much too thin,"

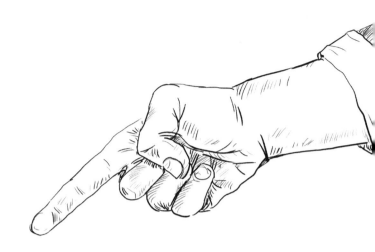

Then, "Maybe you shouldn't have that cookie."

So I said sorry.

They told me, "You're too quiet,"

Then said, "Don't talk so loudly."

So I said sorry.

They suggested, "Don't be shy,"

Then added, "But still be a lady."

So I said sorry.

They urged me to "Aim to be a winner,"

"But don't make anyone else feel lousy."

So I said sorry.

"You should speak your mind," they said;

Then told me, "But don't be bossy."

So I said sorry.

"It's good to ask questions,"

"But start with 'Sorry' or 'Excuse me'."

So I said sorry.

"You say sorry a lot!" they said.

So I said sorry...

... then stopped when I heard myself

Saying "Sorry" for being sorry,

And learned apologizing all the time
Sounds so very silly!

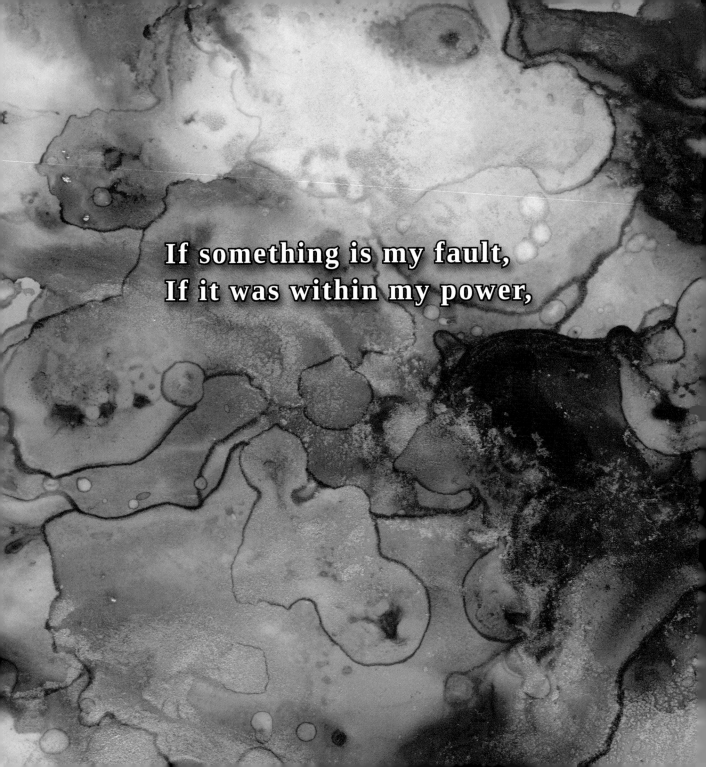

If something is my fault,
If it was within my power,

I will own up to my mistakes
Without ever being sour.

But for my words and choices

That don't hurt anybody else,

I will not say "Sorry"—

They're an expression of myself.

While I want everyone around me
To certainly be happy,

All I can do is be myself
Without apology!

RHYMING
REASON
BOOKS

Books for a stronger and kinder tomorrow.

www.rhymingreason.com

HAYOUNG YIM

is a Third-Wave feminist and writer. More than anything, she believes in effecting social change through popular culture.

This is her first children's book.

She lives in Canada, where she ironically apologizes all the time.

MARTA M.

is an illustrator and graphic designer. Game graphics is her passion, although she has a Master's degree in architecture.

She is located in Poland, where she spends her days designing, loving her cats, and nerding out.

CPSIA information can be obtained at www.ICGtesting.com
Printed in the USA
LVIW01n2034181017
552900LV00001B/7